C0-DME-909

12 STORIES ABOUT
HELPING SENIORS

by Samantha S. Bell

www.12StoryLibrary.com

Copyright © 2020 by 12-Story Library, Mankato, MN 56002. All rights reserved. No part of this book may be reproduced or utilized in any form or by any means without written permission from the publisher.

12-Story Library is an imprint of Bookstaves.

Photographs ©: Motortion Films/Shutterstock.com, cover, 1; 11 Alive/YouTube, 4; 11 Alive/YouTube, 5; Rogers tv/YouTube, 6; Monkey Business Images/Shutterstock.com, 6; Daisy Daisy/Shutterstock.com, 7; National Council on Aging, NPO/PD, 8; Monkey Business Images/Shutterstock.com, 8; Liderina/Shutterstock.com, 9; PD, 10; ALPA PROD/Shutterstock.com, 11; Corporation for National and Community Service/YouTube, 11; DigitalWire360/YouTube, 12; DigitalWire360/YouTube, 13; DOROT/YouTube, 14; DOROT/YouTube, 15; Gawler History/CC2.0, 16; Wellcome Images/CC4.0, 16; Airman 1st Class Katrina Heikkinen/US Air Force, 17; Dwight Burdette/CC3.0, 17; PD, 18; CBS This Morning/YouTube, 19; Jacob Lund/Shutterstock.com, 20; Toa55/Shutterstock.com, 21; Basic Plumbing Repair/YouTube, 21; WTAJ TV/YouTube, 22; sirtravelalot/Shutterstock.com, 22; Africa Studio/Shutterstock.com, 23; AARP/PD, 24; Los Angeles Examiner/University of Southern California/Getty Images, 24; LightField Studios/Shutterstock.com, 25; NM Tech Council/YouTube, 26; 60 Second Docs/YouTube, 27; SpeedKingz/Shutterstock.com, 28; Phovoir/Shutterstock.com, 29

ISBN
9781632357489 (hardcover)
9781632358578 (paperback)
9781645820338 (ebook)

Library of Congress Control Number: 2019938646

Printed in the United States of America
October 2019

About the Cover
A boy shows his grandfather how an app works on his cell phone.

Access free, up-to-date content on this topic plus a full digital version of this book. Scan the QR code on page 31 or use your school's login at 12StoryLibrary.com.

Table of Contents

Three Wishes for Ruby's Residents: Making Wishes Come True . 4

RISE: Fighting Loneliness and Isolation 6

National Council on Aging: Helping Seniors Live Well 8

Beth Patterson and RSVP: Organizing Senior Volunteers 10

Storied Lives: Helping Seniors Tell Their Stories 12

DOROT: Bringing Generations Together 14

Doris Taylor and Meals on Wheels: Hot Meals at Home 16

Giving Voice: Bringing Back Music and Memories 18

CAPABLE: Helping Seniors Age in Place 20

Mojo's Mission: Helping Seniors Care for Their Pets 22

AARP: Serving Seniors in Many Ways 24

Teeniors: Teaching Seniors Tech Skills 26

Ways You Can Help 28

Glossary 30

Read More 31

Index 32

About the Author 32

1

Three Wishes for Ruby's Residents: Making Wishes Come True

Ruby Kate Chitsey in 2019.

Ruby Kate Chitsey was 11 years old when she came up with a way to brighten the lives of many seniors. Chitsey's mother is a nurse. She works in nursing homes near Harrison, Arkansas. In the summer, Chitsey goes to work with her mom. One day, she noticed that a resident named Pearl looked very sad. A pet sitter had brought Pearl's beloved dog in for a visit. But then they left, and Pearl didn't know when she would see her dog again.

Chitsey wanted to help. She knew it cost money to get a pet sitter to bring the dog. She took $12 out of her piggy bank to cover the cost for another visit. Then she thought about the other residents in the nursing home. She wondered how many of them could not afford small things that made them happy.

Chitsey's list turned into a project called Three Wishes for Ruby's Residents. She asked each resident what three things they wished for most of all. She wrote them down in a notebook. The answers surprised Chitsey and her mom. They were not expensive things. Some residents wanted clothes that fit. Some wanted

4

$72,000
Amount of money Ruby Kate Chitsey raised by early 2019

- She began her project at one nursing home.
- Now it includes all five nursing homes where her mom works.
- Chitsey wants her project to expand throughout the United States.

THINK ABOUT IT

Imagine you can't live in your home anymore. You don't have enough money to buy anything extra, and you can't go to the store. What things will you miss most? Why?

new books. One wanted fresh strawberries.

With her mom's help, Chitsey created a Facebook page for her project. She also started an online account for donations. The money goes toward fulfilling the residents' wishes.

Ruby delivers three wishes to a grateful nursing home resident.

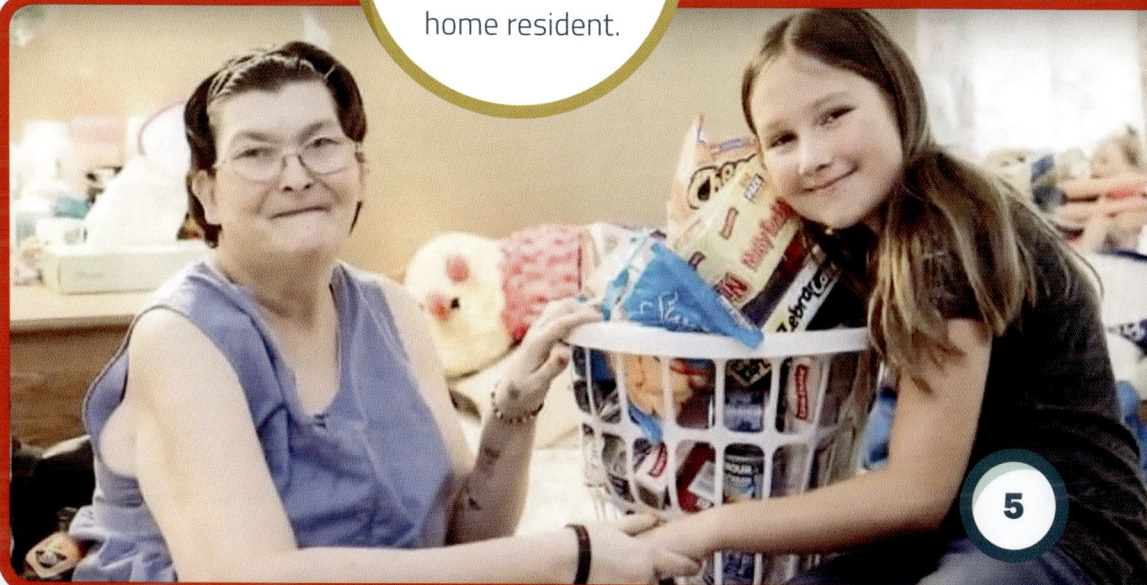

2

RISE: Fighting Loneliness and Isolation

RISE
REACH ISOLATED SENIORS EVERYWHERE

2015
Year when RISE began

- In Canada, over 1 million seniors say they are lonely.
- Individuals and organizations that are helping seniors can report their progress on the RISE website.
- RISE is using social media to spread its message.

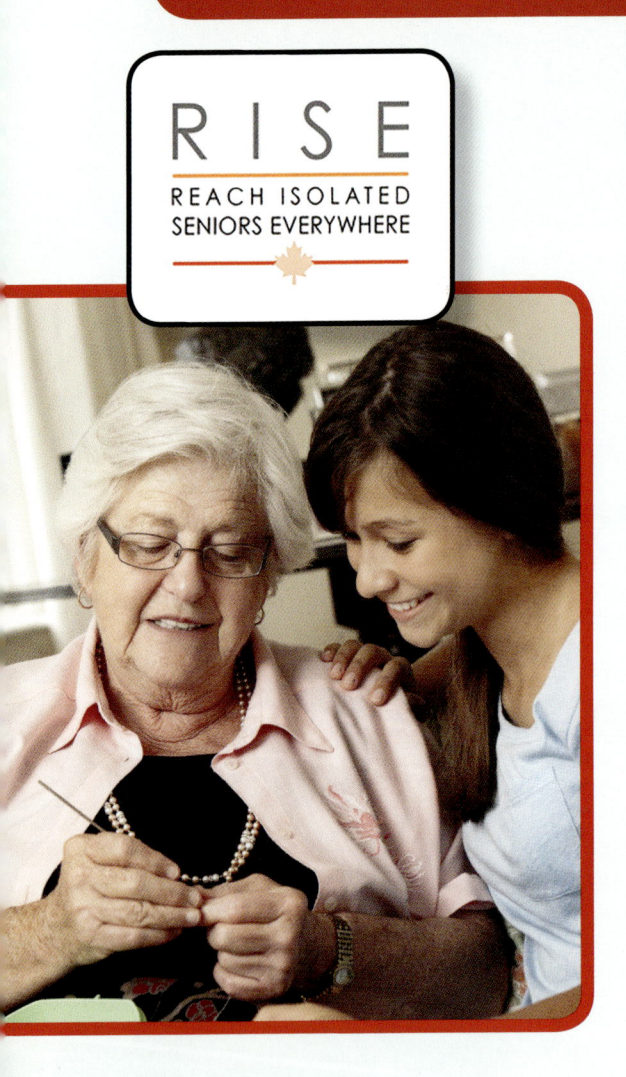

Senior citizens often feel lonely and isolated. Sometimes their children move to another city. Husbands or wives pass away. Often seniors cannot do things like they used to. They may have a hard time getting around. Health problems might keep them indoors. Some seniors can no longer drive. Others don't even have a car.

In Canada, RISE is trying to help. RISE stands for Reach Isolated Seniors Everywhere. It is a national campaign to raise awareness of the

Sharing a meal with a senior helps them feel less lonely.

problem and inspire people to take action. RISE encourages people to reach out to a senior in their own community. This can be a family member, friend, or neighbor.

It doesn't take much to make a difference in the life of a lonely senior. RISE has ideas for people to try. They can call a senior on the phone to say hello. They can go out to eat together or get a cup of coffee. They might take a senior to church, the store, or the library. Any type of social activity can make a senior feel less lonely and more valued.

One of RISE's sayings is "Don't let a senior become 'invisible.'" Each year on a national day called RISE Sunday, RISE asks everyone to contact a senior in their life.

RISE IN WINTER

For many seniors, loneliness becomes worse in winter. The cold weather forces them to stay indoors. RISE reminds people that an act of kindness can warm a winter's day. They can take seniors groceries or medicine. They can stop by just to visit. They can clear seniors' sidewalks of snow.

3

National Council on Aging: Helping Seniors Live Well

The National Council on Aging (NCOA) is an organization that works to improve the lives of people aged 60 and older. It helps seniors stay healthy, secure, and independent. It especially works to help those who don't have a lot of money. To do this, NCOA joins with thousands of other organizations and businesses across the United States. These include senior centers, health centers, and churches. NCOA also partners with government, housing groups, and job services. Together, they provide free services and programs.

One of the programs is called Savvy Saving Seniors. NCOA joined with the Bank of America to create it. The program provides materials communities can use to hold financial workshops for seniors. In the workshops, seniors learn how to budget. They learn how to save money. They also learn how to avoid scams. People can find the

Exercise keeps seniors strong to minimize injury from falls.

materials on NCOA's website and use them for free.

The NCOA also focuses on preventing falls. When seniors fall, they often injure themselves in serious ways. Sometimes they don't recover. The NCOA has programs that can help. One program teaches seniors special exercises. These make them stronger and improve their balance.

The NCOA keeps seniors up-to-date on decisions that will affect them. These include things such as government programs and health care policies. The NCOA offers tips on how people can get involved.

1950
Year when the NCOA was founded

- Over 25 million seniors in the United States are living in poverty.
- As people live longer, this number will grow.
- The NCOA wants to help these seniors live better.

4

Beth Patterson and RSVP: Organizing Senior Volunteers

Beth Patterson in 2019.

When Beth Patterson was growing up, her parents taught her to give back to the community. She started volunteering when she was 12 years old. Older people were kind to her. She discovered she enjoyed working with them. When she went to college, she studied gerontology.

Today Patterson is the director of the Retired and Senior Volunteer Program (RSVP) of Central Oklahoma. RSVP is part of the Corporation for National and Community Service (CNSC), a US government agency. It looks for volunteers aged 55 and older who want to make a difference in their communities. Patterson connects volunteers in Oklahoma with local nonprofit groups. The groups match the volunteers with people and organizations that need their help.

Volunteers can choose from many kinds of opportunities. Some help children with their homework. Others prepare and deliver meals to seniors. Volunteers give support to veterans and their families. They help build homes with Habitat for Humanity.

Many volunteers want a short-term project. Others are willing to make a bigger commitment. Sometimes

GOING PLACES

In 1995, Patterson helped start a new program with RSVP. It is called Provide-a-Ride. Sometimes seniors don't have cars to drive. But they need to get to medical appointments. An RSVP volunteer will pick them up and take them there for free. This way, seniors get the care they need to stay healthy and independent.

160
Number of hours a typical RSVP volunteer contributes each year

- Volunteers work with food banks, hospitals, schools, and libraries.
- Giving back to the community also helps the volunteers.
- They feel what Beth Patterson calls a "helper's high." This is followed by a sense of calm and well-being.

Senior volunteers enjoy helping teens and young children. volunteers are just looking for something to do. Patterson tries to match volunteers with the right opportunities. She wants them to experience the joy and satisfaction of helping others.

5 Storied Lives: Helping Seniors Tell Their Stories

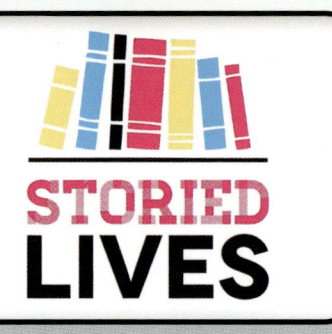

Zeenie Sharif.

High school student Zeenie Sharif enjoyed listening to her grandparents talk about their lives. She thought about other seniors who didn't have family members. They might not have anyone to share their stories with. In 2012, she helped create a program called Storied Lives.

In the program, high school students interview seniors in nursing homes or other care facilities. Then they write short biographies of their seniors. The students honor the seniors by telling their stories.

First, the students complete a short questionnaire. Then each student is matched up with a senior. They may have something in common or similar interests. The students meet the seniors at an opening ceremony.

The seniors are often lonely. But the students spend time with them and get to know them. Most students visit three or four times. They ask the seniors about their lives and things

10
Number of weeks in a typical Storied Lives program

- Storied Lives began in New Jersey.
- It has expanded into many cities across the United States.
- In 2017, the first program started outside the United States, in Australia.

they have done. Then the students write down the stories.

At the end of the program, the stories are given to the seniors at a special closing ceremony. Family members and friends come to the ceremony. The students read the stories they have written. Then they present the stories to the seniors as gifts.

The students learn a lot by writing the stories. They begin to see things in a different way. The seniors enjoy spending time with the students. Some students and seniors become close friends.

A senior having her story read by a student at a closing ceremony.

6

DOROT: Bringing Generations Together

In 1976, a group of students from Columbia University in New York became worried about the older people in the area. Some of the seniors lived in apartments nearby. But they were homebound and often forgotten. The students visited the seniors. They formed close relationships.

They called their group DOROT. This means "generations" in Hebrew. DOROT brought generations together.

Today thousands of DOROT volunteers of all ages are helping seniors. They take them on errands and to doctors' appointments. They go to plays and concerts together. They bring them meals and special holiday food packages. DOROT also provides housing and adult education programs.

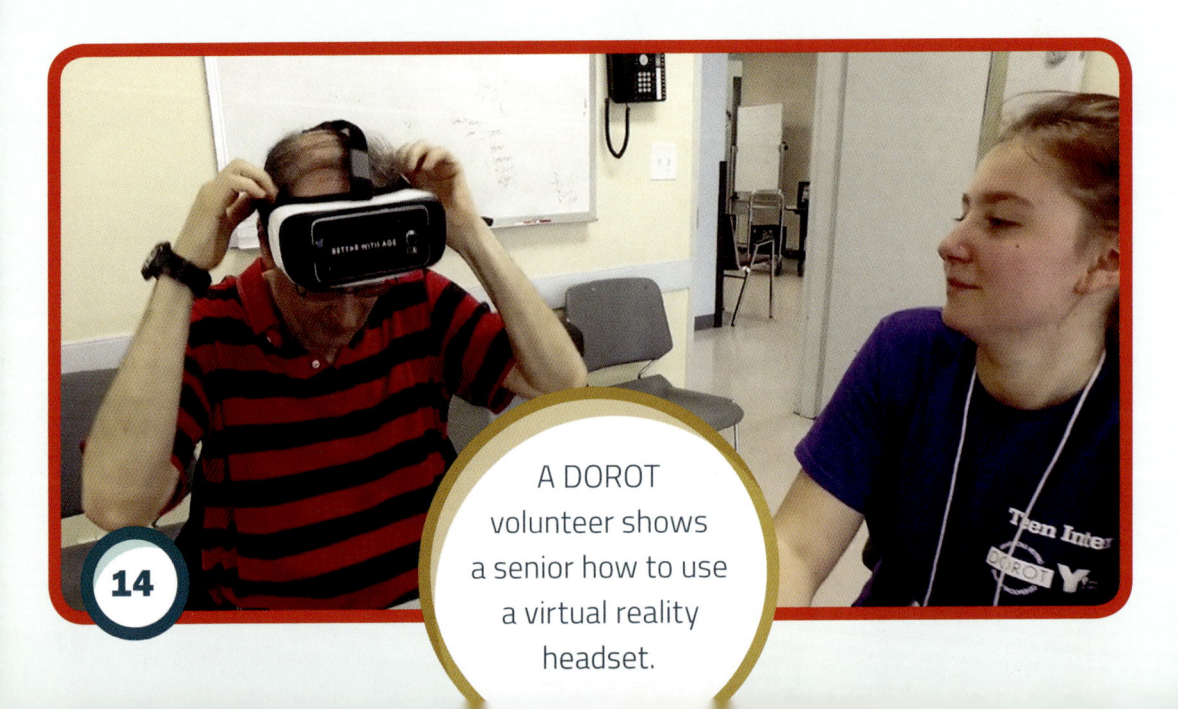

A DOROT volunteer shows a senior how to use a virtual reality headset.

A senior teaches a DOROT volunteer how to knit.

In 2001, DOROT started a summer program for teens. High school students spend the summer working with seniors. They teach them computer skills. They cook and eat with them. They visit the seniors in their homes.

Many times, seniors can feel isolated and alone. By spending time together, DOROT volunteers and seniors form close friendships. For many of the seniors, the volunteers are the only family they have. DOROT is good for the volunteers, too. They benefit from the seniors' wisdom and experience. They feel appreciated.

10,000+
Number of seniors and their caregivers DOROT helps each year

- Many seniors have loved ones who have passed away.
- DOROT volunteers will drive them to the cemetery.
- The volunteers also give comfort and support to people who have lost loved ones.

THINK ABOUT IT
People of different generations can learn from each other. What types of things can you learn from an older friend? What kinds of things could you teach your friend?

7

Doris Taylor and Meals on Wheels: Hot Meals at Home

Doris Taylor (center) celebrating an anniversary of Meals on Wheels in 1966.

Doris Taylor was born in 1901 in Australia. When she was 12 years old, she had a bad fall that left her paralyzed. From then on, she had to use a wheelchair. Doctors told her parents she should live in a special home for people with disabilities. Instead, Taylor returned home to live as independently as she could. But she saw the problems disabled people experience in society.

During the Great Depression of the 1930s, many people were out of work. Taylor became concerned about the poor in her community. She worried about families with children. She raised money for food and clothes. After World War II (1939–1945), she began to focus on senior citizens and people with disabilities. She wanted to figure out a way they could stay in their homes.

Meals on Wheels

16

A volunteer delivers a Thanksgiving dinner to a Meals on Wheels recipient.

MEALS IN AMERICA

Meals on Wheels America also began in 1954. Seniors today can choose from a variety of hot or cold meals. The meals are delivered by volunteers who fill another important need. They visit the seniors every day. This helps keep the seniors from feeling lonely and isolated.

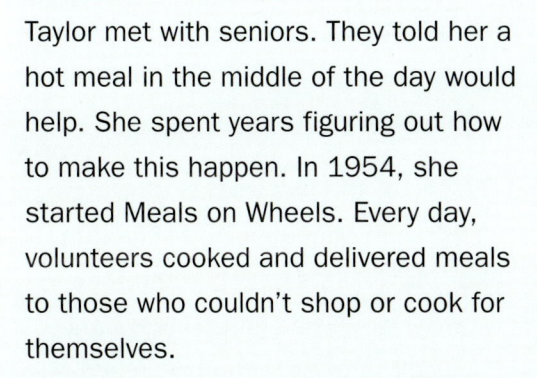

Taylor met with seniors. They told her a hot meal in the middle of the day would help. She spent years figuring out how to make this happen. In 1954, she started Meals on Wheels. Every day, volunteers cooked and delivered meals to those who couldn't shop or cook for themselves.

Taylor's Meals on Wheels program is still going strong. People who receive the meals pay only a small amount for the food.

11

Number of volunteers who delivered South Australia's first Meals on Wheels

- The meals were cooked in the Meals on Wheels kitchen in Port Adelaide.
- Individuals and businesses donated money and equipment for the kitchen.
- Today Meals on Wheels in South Australia has approximately 8,000 volunteers.

8

Giving Voice: Bringing Back Music and Memories

Mary Lenard (left) and Marge Ostroushko.

giving voice

Alzheimer's is a disease that destroys memory and thinking skills. Both Mary Lenard and Marge Ostroushko have personal experience with Alzheimer's in their families. They heard how music can help people with the disease. Music involves more parts of the brain than other types of memory. Some of these parts are not affected by memory loss. People with Alzheimer's often remember how to sing. They remember music from their past.

In 2014, the two women started a chorus in Minneapolis, Minnesota, for Alzheimer's patients and their caregivers. The chorus meets once a week. Anyone with Alzheimer's or other kinds of memory loss can join, along with the people who take care of them. No musical experience or training is needed.

TRYING SOMETHING NEW

In 2018, Giving Voice Chorus took on a new challenge. They sang a concert with nine original songs. A composer and a poet wrote the songs just for them. Even the members with memory loss were able to learn the new songs.

The music helps the patients think and focus. They may recover some of their memory. Singing also brings them joy. No one is worried about making mistakes. Many patients look forward to the days they get to sing.

The chorus is also a way to connect with others. Caregivers can give each other support and encouragement. Patients can visit with other people. While they are singing, patients and caregivers feel like equals again. They are just people enjoying the same experience.

30
Number of people who came to the first Giving Voice rehearsal

- Giving Voice has gone worldwide. Today there are choruses across the United States and in the United Kingdom.
- Anyone can start a chorus.
- Giving Voice offers free directions on their website for how to start a chorus.

Some Alzheimer's patients recover memories from singing.

9

CAPABLE: Helping Seniors Age in Place

As most people age, they still want to live in their own homes. They don't want to move to assisted living or senior housing. They want to remain independent. But sometimes it's hard. They may need extra help. This costs money some seniors don't have. They start feeling they can't make it on their own anymore. They may get depressed.

John Hopkins School of Nursing developed a program to help low-income seniors age in place. Aging in place means being able to stay in your own home and community as you get older. The program is called CAPABLE.

Each senior in the program is assigned a nurse, an occupational therapist, and a handyman. They ask what the senior wants to be able to do. Many seniors want to cook their own meals. Some want to be able to make their own

Nurses learn what seniors need in order to continue living independently.

beds. Others want to go out and get around on their own. The nurse and therapist figure out ways to make these things easier to do. The handyman makes the senior's home safer and easier to manage.

With CAPABLE, seniors can do more things on their own. Some can go grocery shopping again. Others can manage their medicine. They feel better about themselves. Many show fewer signs of depression.

> Grab bars allow seniors to live independently and more safely at home.

5
Number of months a senior is involved with CAPABLE

- CAPABLE stands for Community Aging in Place—Advancing Better Living for Elders.
- The nurse makes four visits. The occupational therapist makes six visits. The handyman does a full day's work.
- The seniors don't have to pay for anything.

AN EXTRA BENEFIT

Besides helping seniors, CAPABLE saves money. When people feel better about themselves, they take better care of themselves. This saves money on medical care. One study showed that CAPABLE helped save about $10,000 a year per senior in health care costs.

10 Mojo's Mission: Helping Seniors Care for Their Pets

Anne Trexler in 2019.

Anne Trexler and her daughters have rescued many animals. Today they are helping both pets and their senior owners through an outreach program called Mojo's Mission.

Trexler and her daughters live in Pennsylvania. They deliver meals to seniors in the area. One of the seniors had three dogs. She wasn't able to care for all of them. That's when Trexler realized there was a need in her community. Working with Mojo's Mission, she stepped in to help.

Caring for a pet can be difficult. Some seniors don't have much money for pet food or vet bills. Seniors can also have health problems that make it hard to clean up after a pet. They may not be able to take their pets on walks. But many seniors rely on their pets for companionship and comfort.

Mojo's Mission volunteers help owners with their dogs, cats, and birds. The program assigns one volunteer to each senior. The volunteers help in different ways. Some feed the pets. Others take

Mojo's Mission volunteers help seniors keep their pets healthy.

them to appointments at the vet. They take them to be groomed. They bring the owners donations of pet food and other supplies.

IN MEMORY OF MOJO

Mojo was a Chihuahua. He had an elderly owner who lived by herself. She developed Alzheimer's and forgot to feed him. When someone finally found him, he was very sick. He wasn't able to recover, and he died. But people saw the need to help, and Mojo's Mission was created.

2019
Year when Mojo's Mission began helping seniors

- Mojo's Mission started as part of the Mia Foundation, a group that rescues animals with birth defects.
- The program plans to expand across the United States.
- Volunteers work hard to keep the pets happy, healthy, and home.

23

11

AARP: Serving Seniors in Many Ways

AARP® Real Possibilities

38 million
Approximate number of AARP members

- Some AARP members volunteer with the AARP Experience Corps.
- AARP trains the volunteers to help children with reading.
- The volunteers work with students in grades K through 3 to improve their reading skills.

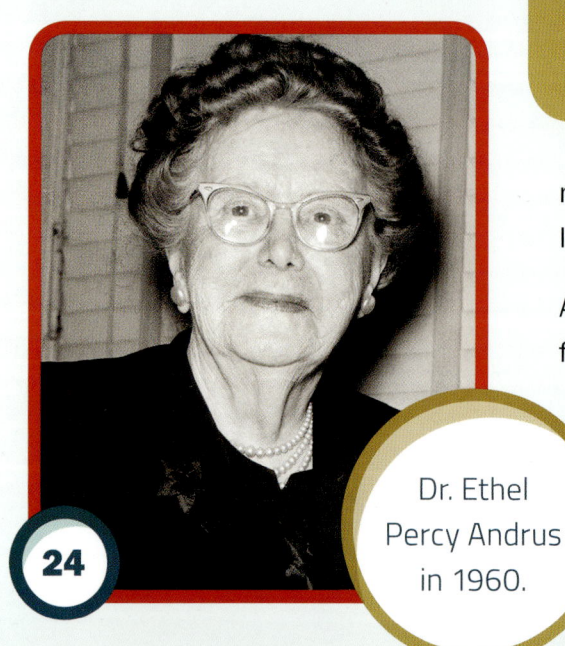

Dr. Ethel Percy Andrus was the first female school principal in California. After she retired, she worked for the California Retired Teachers Association. She realized some older Americans were in trouble. They did not have enough money or health insurance. They felt like they were no longer useful.

Andrus wanted to help. In 1958, she founded the American Association of Retired Persons. Today it is known as AARP. The organization works to help people aged 50 and over.

Dr. Ethel Percy Andrus in 1960.

24

The AARP Silver Sneakers program helps seniors maintain strength for their daily activities.

Members pay a small fee each year. Then they receive discounts on many different products and services. They can pay less for auto and health insurance. They can also save money when they travel. AARP members get discounts on hotels, cruises, and airplane tickets. Restaurants offer discounts, too. Members can also save money on groceries, electronics, and clothing.

Some seniors belong to AARP's Silver Sneakers program. As part of the program, they can use certain gyms for free. They can also take group fitness classes. The workouts are designed just for seniors. They help increase strength for daily activities. They are safe for all fitness levels.

AARP supports seniors in other ways, too. Workers go to Washington, DC. They talk to members of Congress. They encourage them to pass laws that will help older Americans.

12

Teeniors: Teaching Seniors Tech Skills

Trish Lopez worked as a teacher for 30 years. Then she decided to start something new. She wanted to help seniors with technology. She knew that young people know a lot about it. Lopez created Teeniors, a program based in New Mexico. The program brings tech-savvy teens together with seniors. The teens teach the seniors about their devices and how to use them.

Many seniors aren't comfortable with technology. They may be afraid to use the internet. Teens coach the seniors one-on-one. They focus on each senior's specific needs. They help them with smartphones and computers. They show them how to use new software programs. They give them tips for staying safe online. They teach them how to create and use different passwords for their accounts.

The teens also show the seniors how to use technology to stay connected with loved ones. Seniors learn to FaceTime with their children or grandchildren. They might use

Trish Lopez in 2017.

A Teenior volunteer helps a senior with computer skills.

social media to keep up with friends and family members. They may want to use email to stay in touch or share photos.

Some seniors pay for the service. But even if they can't pay, teens are still available to help. Donations help cover the costs for seniors who don't have much money.

2015
Year when Teeniors began

- Teeniors coaches range in age from 16 to 29.
- Teachers and parents recommend teens for the program.
- The program provides meaningful work for teens.

THINK ABOUT IT

Teeniors share their tech skills with seniors. What tech skills do you have? How would you teach one or more of those skills to a senior?

27

Ways You Can Help

- Get together with friends and find out about nursing homes and senior care facilities in your community. Ask an adult to help you plan a visit.

- If you have a friendly dog or cat, maybe you can bring it along. You'll have to get permission.

- Make a card for an elderly friend or neighbor. Go with a parent or guardian to deliver it in person.

- Teach a senior something new about their smartphone or computer.

- Ask a senior to tell you about their childhood. You might start with questions like "Where did you grow up?" "Did you have any brothers or sisters?" "What was your favorite thing to do when you were my age?"

- Help your parents or guardians deliver Meals on Wheels.

- Take a walk with an older neighbor or relative. If you live near a park, bring a snack to share. Sit on a park bench and talk for a while.

- Help a senior with yard work such as weeding or mowing the lawn.

- Call a senior family member to say hello. Ask how their day was. Talk about your day.

- Invite a senior to a play or concert at your school.

Glossary

budget
To make a plan for using money.

generation
A group of people born and living at the same time.

gerontology
The scientific study of old age and the problems that come with growing older.

homebound
Unable to leave one's house, especially because of old age or illness.

isolated
Having little contact with other people.

nonprofit
An organization that does not make money from its work.

occupational therapist
A person who helps patients recover or improve skills needed for daily activities, such as getting dressed, cooking, and eating.

paralyzed
When part of the body is unable to move.

questionnaire
A set of printed questions for the purpose of gathering information.

scam
A way to make money by cheating people.

short-term
Something that happens over a brief period of time.

Read More

Ancona, George. *Can We Help? Kids Volunteering to Help Their Communities.* Sommerville, MA: Candlewick Press, 2015.

Love, Ann, and Jane Drake. *Kids and Grandparents: An Activity Book.* Toronto, Ontario: Kids Can Press, 1999.

Orr, Tamra. *Ways to Help the Elderly.* Hallandale Beach, FL: Mitchell Lane Publishers, 2010.

Visit 12StoryLibrary.com

Scan the code or use your school's login at **12StoryLibrary.com** for recent updates about this topic and a full digital version of this book. Enjoy free access to:

- Digital ebook
- Breaking news updates
- Live content feeds
- Videos, interactive maps, and graphics
- Additional web resources

Note to educators: Visit 12StoryLibrary.com/register to sign up for free premium website access. Enjoy live content plus a full digital version of every 12-Story Library book you own for every student at your school.

Index

American Association of Retired Persons, (AARP), 24-25

budgeting, 8, 30

CAPABLE, 20-21
caring for pets, 22-23
Chitsey, Ruby Kate, 4-5

delivering, 5, 17
DOROT, 14-15

exercising, 9, 25

Giving Voice, 18-19

health care, 9, 21

independent living, 8, 11, 16, 20-21

Meals on Wheels, 16-17
Mojo's Mission, 22-23

National Council on Aging (NCOA), 8-9

Patterson, Beth, 10-11

raising money, 5, 16
Reach Isolated Seniors Everywhere (RISE), 6-7
receiving discounts, 24-25

Retired Senior Volunteer Program (RSVP), 10-11

singing, 18-19
Storied Lives, 12-13

Taylor, Doris, 16-17
teaching, 15, 26-27
Teeniors, 26-27
Three Wishes for Ruby's Residents, 4-5

visiting, 7, 12, 14-15, 17, 28

ways to help, 28-29
writing, 12-13

About the Author
Samantha S. Bell lives in upstate South Carolina with her family and lots of animals. She is the author of more than 100 nonfiction books for children.

READ MORE FROM 12-STORY LIBRARY

Every 12-Story Library Book is available in many fomats. For more information, visit 12StoryLibrary.com